CHASING A SPECTRE

BOOK ZERO OF THE WAR FOR DOMINANCE

Chris Kennedy

Chris Kennedy Publishing

Virginia Beach, VA

Chris Kennedy/Chris Kennedy Publishing
2052 Bierce Dr.
Virginia Beach, VA 23454
http://chriskennedypublishing.com/

Publisher's Note: This is a work of fiction. Names, characters, places, and incidents are a product of the author's imagination. Locales and public names are sometimes used for atmospheric purposes. Any resemblance to actual people, living or dead, or to businesses, companies, events, institutions, or locales is completely coincidental.

Ordering Information:
Quantity sales. Special discounts are available on quantity purchases by corporations, associations, and others. For details, contact the "Special Sales Department" at the address above.

Can't Look Back/ Chris Kennedy. – 1st ed.
ISBN 978-1942936022

As always, this book is for my wife and children. I would like to thank Linda, Beth, Dan and Jimmy, who took the time to critically read the work and make it better. Any mistakes that remain are my own. I would like to thank my mother, without whose steadfast belief in me, I would not be where I am today. Thank you.

Chapter One:
The Poor Quarter

"The Spectre went through there," panted Dantes, pointing at a mirror at the end of the alley. The mirror's surface shimmered once and then seemed to solidify before their eyes.

Ghorza slowed to a walk as she approached it. The mirror's glass made a 'plink' noise as the metal end of her staff tapped it, but remained otherwise unresponsive. "Well, whatever magic he used to go through it has already dissipated," she replied, breathing heavily. The mirror appeared unremarkable amidst the refuse at the end of the dark alley. "It looks like a normal mirror now."

"Wonderful," sighed Dantes, his breathing a little more under control. He wasn't known for his speed and endurance; chasing the thief had taken a lot out of him. A teufling, Dantes had a devil in his lineage, which showed through in his brick-red skin, thick horns and prehensile tail. The purple eyes were especially disconcerting to look into, even if they did match his purple hair.

Dantes pointed at the imitation gem stones that surrounded the glass on all four sides of the mirror. "There's got to be at least 70 gems there. If it's a four gem spell, there's no way that we're ever going to figure out the pattern. We were really close to catching the Spectre this time, but it looks like he's gotten away."

"Again," added Ghorza. A half-orc, she was an outsider anywhere she went, in human lands or orc. As if the pale green skin and tusked teeth didn't set her apart enough on their own, the tufts of coarse hair covering her body made finding human companionship impossible unless she went to the taverns at closing time. Even then, she didn't always get lucky...and no one stayed in the morning.

Ghorza reached over to stroke the mirror, as if her hand could absorb the secret pattern necessary to activate the mirror's travel spell. "Let's get back to the Magistra," she said, referring to the head of their order. "She will want to know what's happened, even though we failed to catch the thief or find the queen's crown. Bring the mirror. Maybe she knows a spell that will show us which gems he used to activate it. If nothing else, at least he won't be able to use it to travel again."

"Don't you think the Spectre would have put a spell on it to keep that kind of magic from working?" asked Dantes.

Now it was Ghorza's turn to sigh. The teufling always seemed to think things through better than she did, even though he wasn't able to use magic as well. "Yeah, he probably did," Ghorza said. "Still, we need to bring it back so he can't travel back through it again. Besides, what can it hurt to bring it back?"

"Besides my back carrying it?" grumbled Dantes. "Nothing." He shook his head in frustration. "I really thought we had him this time, too. I'd pay all of the money I had to my name if we could get this mirror to work."

"Really?" asked a thin voice from the darkness of the alleyway's corner. "And how much would that be?"

Ghorza's head snapped around. "Who's there?" she demanded. "Come out *now*, before we blast you with a fireball!"

"Such force is hardly necessary," said the voice. "I surrender."

Ghorza and Dantes looked down in shock. The voice came from a little gray mouse that swaggered up to them and bowed. "So," it asked again, "how much are you willing to pay for the combination to the mirror?"

Chapter Two:
Institute for the Arcane

"We will discuss this in council and put together a team to go into the mirror after the thief," said the Magistra. A snow elf, the Magistra was taller and wirier than most elves, standing almost three inches above six feet, with the light brown skin, long white hair, silver eyes and pointed ears that were common to her race. Typical of elves in general, who lived centuries the way humans lived decades, she was also slow to come to a decision.

"But we've got to go after him now!" exclaimed Ghorza, who came to decisions far more quickly. "He has the queen's crown! The longer we delay, the further away he could be getting!"

Milos shook his head. A halfling, he looked human but was only three and a half feet tall. "The delay is unacceptable," he said, interrupting the mages' discussion.

"What do you mean?" asked the Magistra.

"I saw him go through the gate," he said, "and I know there is a reward for his capture." A beast master who could use magic to project his senses into animals, Milos had been controlling the mouse in the alley. "How many times have these two already failed to capture him?" he asked. "We can't afford to give him a head start. We need to go through the mirror *now* to make sure he doesn't get away. I might have caught him myself this time if the tuefy hadn't come stomping along and spooked him." He narrowed his eyes and looked at Dantes.

"*You* would have caught him?" asked Dantes with a glare of his own. "As a mouse, how would you have accomplished the task? By giving him rabies and waiting for him to die?"

"I would have gone back to my body and grabbed him," mumbled Milos, finding something interesting on the ground to stare at.

"*You* would have grabbed him?" asked Dantes, eyeing the much smaller and weaker Milos. "How? Most reports say he is a big man."

"They also say he is a master of disguise," said the Magistra. "Did you get a good look at him?"

"He wasn't that much larger than I am," replied Milos. "In fact, I was about to grab him when he heard you coming. It's almost as if...as if you didn't want to catch the thief at all. That's it!" he exclaimed, turning to the Magistra. "No wonder they can't catch the thief. The devil is probably helping him."

Anger blazed through Dantes, and flames began to dance on his skin. Within seconds, the smell of charred material filled the room. Even though his clothes were treated and warded, there was only so much that 'fireproof' could do when covering skin that often burst into open flames.

"Say that again, pig lover, and you'll see what it's like to be roasted in your own juices!" Dantes warned. "I have *never* done anything to help the thief!"

"*Calm yourself!*" said the Magistra. "Remember your training and your oath."

Because of his parentage, Ghorza knew that Dantes had to swear not one, but several oaths in order for the Magistra to take him in, including his vows to pray only to the gods of good and to practice good wherever he went. More to the point, he had also sworn to abstain from torture in all forms and to never kill anyone, except in the line of duty.

Dantes took several deep breaths the way he had been taught, wisps of smoke trailing from his nostrils as he exhaled.

"Yes, Magistra," he finally replied. "I remember my training and all of my oaths. It is because I *have* been true to my oaths that this dirt crawler riles me by saying that I am a thief, or that I help thieves. It has been hard enough to get people around here to accept me, and if that rumor gets out, I will lose the support of the few that *do* trust me."

"I understand," said the Magistra. She looked at Milos and said, "Perhaps it would be better for all of us if you watched your tongue. While we would like your assistance, it will be hard to get it from you if you are fried to a crisp."

Milos simply nodded, saying nothing. After a few seconds, he looked at Ghorza and raised an eyebrow.

Ghorza understood his unspoken question; as a half-orc, she was as much an outcast as Dantes. "You're just as liable to come to an untimely end if you accuse me as you would be if you continued to accuse Dantes," she said, glaring down at Milos. Ghorza was a practitioner of air-based magic. Although young, she was a talented magician; her threat wasn't an idle one.

"All I want is my reward," whined Milos, turning to look imploringly again at the Magistra. When Milos had come out from where he had been hiding in the alley, Ghorza had been unimpressed with him. So far, nothing had changed. The halfling looked like he spent half of his day digging in a garbage heap and the other half rolling around in a manure pile. Ghorza had heard that beast masters often ended up no better than the creatures they controlled; they simply became inured to the animals' constant filth. She hadn't believed it before…but she believed it now.

"So far you haven't done anything to deserve a reward," the Magistra replied.

"True," agreed Milos, "but that's because I didn't want them to sneak off with the mirror's combination, never to be heard from again. Maybe the mirror leads to a land of wealth, where gold rests at the bottom of every river, just waiting to be picked up. They might never have come back, and I would never have received my reward. I heard the king offered 100 pieces of gold for information that led to the capture of the Spectre and the return of the crown. I want to make sure that my claim doesn't get lost or forgotten."

"My word is law," replied the Magistra, "and I say that if you give us the combination, and if these two go through and bring back the thief, then I will ensure that your claim is paid."

"There are a lot of 'ifs' in that sentence," remarked Milos. He looked down at his clothes as if for the first time. "This reward could change my life. 100 gold pieces is more than I would make in ten years of finding people's lost pets and bringing their kittens down from trees. I could actually bathe for once and sit at the bar in the mead hall, rather than always eating outside with the swine and cattle."

That plea fell on deaf ears with both Ghorza and Dantes, who often had to eat outside with the livestock. Boo hoo, Ghorza thought, life is tough all over.

"The biggest 'if,'" continued Milos, "is 'if they bring back the thief,' something that they have been unable to do so far. How many times has the Spectre struck, and these two failed to apprehend him? Six? Seven times now? So many now that he has become bold enough to steal the queen's own crown? I don't foresee them bringing him back this time, either. He went to great pains to cover his tracks; there's no telling what his escape plan was once he went through the mirror. For all we know, he has another mirror that he used to come right back into this world from whatever time and place he went."

"It's only been five times," said Dantes. "The first two don't count because we weren't involved then."

"OK, five times," allowed Milos. "They've had plenty of chances and have failed every time. If they are going through the mirror, I want to go too, so that I can watch out for my interests. I'll make sure they come back with both the thief and my reward."

"No way," replied Ghorza. "I don't want him coming with us. He'll only get in the way. And he smells."

"*I* smell?" Milos shrieked. "You're obviously so used to your own reek that you don't notice it any more. I could smell you coming a long way off."

"You *are* somewhat...fragrant, Ghorza," agreed the Magistra. "Besides, Milos has talents that might help you catch the thief. He could use a dog to track the thief without having to go to the local authorities. We don't know what they use for payment, but it is unlikely our coins will work there." She paused. "Yes," she said, deciding, "you two will go through the mirror, and you will take Milos with you."

"So I can go?" Milos asked. The Magistra nodded her head. After a second, Dantes did, too. Ghorza looked like she had bitten into something sour, but finally nodded her head.

"And I'll get my reward when we return with the thief?" The Magistra nodded again. "In that case," he said, "the combination is the blue gem in the upper left, the red gem in the lower right, the green gem in the upper right and the yellow gem in the lower left, in that order. Those were the stones that the thief pushed, and in the order that he pushed them."

"You must have been close to see that," said Ghorza. "Did you get a good look at his face?"

"Unfortunately, no," replied Milos. "I was concentrating on what he was doing, and he had his hood pulled down low over his face, making it difficult to see him. I did hear his voice, though, and I will recognize it if I hear it again. You'll appreciate this; he said, 'A half-orc and a half-devil will never catch me. They're both half-wits.' If we can find him, I'll know him by his voice."

* * *

Three hours later, the trio was ready to depart.

Dantes eyed the scimitar at Ghorza's side. Although it wasn't illegal for a mage to carry a sword, it was almost as uncommon as it was for the sun to rise from the south. It just wasn't done. Dantes could tell this wasn't the first time she had worn it, either; the leather scabbard was well worn in all the right places.

Ghorza saw where he was looking and shrugged. "A girl gets less abuse on the road," she explained, "if it looks like she can defend herself."

Dantes knew that a man would have to be awfully hard up to feel like giving a half-orc woman 'any abuse' in the first place. He also knew that it was...impractical...to mention that fact to any woman, much less Ghorza, so he nodded sagely as if he understood and agreed.

Having dealt with the question, Ghorza turned to the Magistra. "Does the Council have any guidance for us?" she asked.

"Yes," said the Magistra. "The Council has decided to exile him. If you can recover the stolen goods and ensure that he doesn't have another means of transportation back to this world, you are authorized to leave him there. When you get back, we will break the mirror, trapping him wherever he is for all time." She looked speculatively at Ghorza. "Personally, I would advise you to have a Translate spell ready, in case you hadn't already thought of that. You might come out of the mirror somewhere close by, but you may also end up far enough away from here that they speak a different language."

"Uh yeah, I was going to do that," said Ghorza, who knew that she should have thought of that herself...but hadn't.

Ghorza could tell the Magistra saw through her statement. The smile that she gave Ghorza was only on her lips. Her silver eyes told Ghorza that she needed to act less and think more. Just like always. Ghorza vowed, once again, that this time she would.

Chapter Three:
Into the Unknown

Ghorza activated the mirror, stepping out onto a small platform in a room with several stalls. It was brighter than any indoor room she had ever seen, with some sort of light spell burning behind a screen in the ceiling. To judge by the smell, something had recently defecated nearby. Either that or it had died; her money was on the creature's death. Before she had a chance to survey her surroundings further, Dantes stepped through the mirror, nearly knocking her off the platform. She stumbled slightly as she realized that the platform wasn't flat; it had several round depressions in it, with metal pieces that hung over them. She had no idea what they were, but if they were decorations, they weren't very impressive.

"Careful, you big oaf," she said as Dantes jostled her again, nearly knocking her into one of the cut out areas.

As they both tried to regain their balance, the door into the room opened at the end of the platform, and a large bipedal creature came in. Dark-skinned and bald, it was the ugliest creature Ghorza ever had the misfortune to lay eyes upon, with large, ridged furrows of skin across the top of its head. It was also very fierce and warlike in appearance, causing Dantes to begin casting a flame strike spell.

Before he could hurl it at the stranger, the creature shook its head and said something as it started back out the door. *"Convertite,"*

Ghorza ordered, casting a Translate spell. She caught the creature's last few words.

"Really?" it said as it walked out. "On the counter? Couldn't you guys get a room?" It shook its head again as the door shut. As it walked away, she could just barely hear it say, "And they say Klingons are freaks."

Milos chose that moment to walk through the mirror, bumping into Dantes, who in turn knocked Ghorza off the platform onto the floor, three feet below. "*Natate*," she commanded, casting a cushion spell to help her land softly.

Smaller than the teufling, Milos bounced off him to the side. He fell onto the platform, with his right foot ending up in one of the depressions. The metal piece proved to be a pipe, as water came spurting out of it, drenching his felt shoe.

"Just my luck," he sighed. "Now I have to walk around squelching all day. And what is that smell? Did something *die?*"

"No," replied Dantes. "I think we're in a very large outhouse,"

"Really?" asked Ghorza. "Then what are those white things hanging on the wall over there?"

"I believe those are for men to urinate in," Dantes explained.

"But, you would have to be standing...um...never mind," Ghorza trailed off, her skin beginning to tinge a darker shade of green. Dantes smiled; it was rare to embarrass Ghorza.

"It's not an outhouse," corrected Milos, who had opened the door a crack and was peering out. "We're inside a large building."

"Interesting," Dantes said, pushing open one of the stall doors. He walked into the stall and looked critically at the white porcelain structure for a few seconds before shrugging his shoulders. "Aside from the smell in here, there is no evidence that this is an outhouse. I wonder if someone cleans out these bowls."

As Dantes left the stall, there was a loud 'wooosh' from behind him. He turned around in time to see all the water empty and then refill. "Water magic," he said, nodding his head. "The water is trained to know when you are using it, and when you are done. At that time, it removes your waste to the manure pile."

He walked over to the shelf with the depressions in it and held his hands under the metal piece where the water had run over Milos' shoe. Once again, water poured out of the metal tube. "How thoughtful," he added. "A place to get water for your familiar."

"Hurray, that's wonderful," remarked Milos from the door. "However, neither of you have familiars, so what's the point? You need to come and see what's going on outside of this inside outhouse. You're never going to believe this."

The two junior wizards walked to the door, and Milos opened it further so that all three could look out. The riot of color and noise on the other side of the door was unlike anything they had ever seen. There were a good number of elves, at least five of the Klingons and a few members from several other races. The majority of the people that could be seen were humans, and most of them were dressed in a manner unlike anything the group had ever seen before.

"I've travelled throughout most of Tasidar," said Dantes, "and I've never seen people that dressed like that. Nor have I ever seen a building that looks like this."

"Neither have I," said Ghorza. Most of the people they could see had trousers that were cut above their knees, showing most of the skin of their legs. Scandalous! "If they wore that where I grew up, most of them would be raped repeatedly. The men as well as the women."

"This must be a very mercantile society," mused Dantes. "I can't read what it says on their tunics, but nearly all of them are advertising something."

Ghorza looked down at her own clothes, comparing them to what she was seeing. "Our clothes are different than what most of the people here are wearing; however, there are enough wearing similar things that we ought to be able to pass as locals without arousing too much suspicion."

"Except for these," said Milos, rubbing one of Dantes' horns. "I don't see any demon spawn out there."

Dantes slapped Milos' hand away. "You're going to see a demon spawn's fist if you touch me again."

"Easy," said Ghorza. She pursed her lips as she gazed out the door. "Perhaps we should split up and search this building to see what we can find. Let's meet back here in an hour."

"That's fine with me," Dantes agreed. "If I have to stay near Milos much longer, I am afraid I will forget my vows. Then again, in this new place, I wonder if the vows still hold..."

"Wouldn't it be easier to use magic?" asked Milos, changing the subject. "Couldn't you just teleport us to the Spectre?"

"No," said Ghorza. "I don't have a group Teleport spell. That is a higher level spell than I can currently cast. Besides, I'd be afraid to use it here. Something feels weird with the magic."

"What do you mean, 'feels weird with the magic,'" asked Dantes. "I haven't noticed anything wrong with it."

"That's because you haven't cast anything yet," explained Ghorza. "There's not as much magic here. It took my manna longer to refill after I cast the cantrip than I have ever felt before. Not only is there less magic here, but what exists is less potent. If you cast anything greater than a second-level spell, you won't be able to recharge and do it again anytime soon. I don't know if I'll be able to use that Translate spell again today. It's a good thing I have two."

"*Scintilla!*" commanded Dantes. A spark shot from his pointer claw.

"I see what you mean," agreed Dantes. The void in his manna took more than four times as long to refill than it would have at home. "If even a cantrip takes that long to refill, real spells are going to take days to refill...maybe even weeks, depending on the level."

"Exactly!" said Ghorza. "Like I said, there is less magic here, and it is less potent, as well."

Dantes frowned. "That bodes ill for us. We will have to use our minds and not our magic to the greatest extent possible." That worried him, as Ghorza was too impulsive with her magic for his taste. Normally, her magic refilled more quickly than anyone else he knew; she would often throw spells without thinking, knowing that she would be able to cast them again in no time. The warning was spoken for her benefit, not because he had come up with some earth-shattering insight, but because he was hoping to restrain her profligacy.

Seeing that Ghorza wasn't going to argue, Dantes added, "We'll also have to use our feet. Let's go take a look around. We'll meet back here in an hour."

* * *

"Did anyone find anything?" Ghorza asked an hour later, after they had reunited.

"Beside lots of strange people doing strange things and talking in a strange language?" asked Milos. "No, I didn't."

"I found the merchant's quarter," said Ghorza. "There was a giant room, with all manner of people selling all sorts of things."

"Was one of those things lunch?" asked Milos. "I'm really hungry."

"No," replied Ghorza. "None of those things was lunch." She reached into her traveling bag. "I did, however, purchase you each one of the local tunics, what they call 't-shirts,' so that you can blend in."

"How did you pay for that?" asked Dantes, who knew it would take more than one of the local tunics for him to blend in. A lot more. "Do they take our coins?"

"I used an Obscure spell," Ghorza replied. "The merchants thought they were receiving their own coins, but they were ours."

Dantes shook his head at her unnecessary use of magic. She would never learn. "Well, I found something," he related, "as well as a lot of people who wanted to touch my horns."

"You didn't kill anyone, I hope?" inquired Ghorza, knowing how much he hated that. She had rubbed them once when they first met. She still had the scar to prove it.

"No, although many of them deserved it," he replied. His shoulders twitched in a small shrug. "Follow me; I will show you what I found."

They walked into one of the larger rooms, pushing their way through the throng. The noise the crowd made in the enclosed area rivaled the clamor of the animal pens at a slaughterhouse. The people didn't smell much better, either. The group worked its way across the room to a corner that held a large square of parchment-like material, with squiggles covering most of its surface.

"I think that this may be some sort of directory for what is going on here," Dantes noted. "While I was walking around, I saw many people come by this board, point at something and then walk away quickly in a new direction. Although we don't have much magic here, I think that casting a Read Languages spell on it might help us determine where to start our search."

"I'm willing to try it," agreed Ghorza, thinking ahead for once, "but I only have one of them memorized. I probably won't be able to cast it again today."

"I think it's a risk we have to take," replied Dantes.

"We need to do something," agreed Milos. "He could be anywhere by now."

Ghorza closed her eyes for a second. When she opened them again, she commanded, "*Videamus*," and pointed her finger at the sheet.

Before their eyes, the letters took on a life of their own, the words disassembling and reassembling of their own volition. "FanCon," the document read, "A Convention Dedicated to Fantasy in All its Forms."

Dantes scanned the document quickly, hoping to find something before the spell ended. "By the five gods of good!" he exclaimed. "It's the Spectre!"

"What?" asked Ghorza, who had always been a slower reader. "Where?"

Dantes pointed to one of the events.

"Costuming 101," Ghorza read. "How to appear as someone or something you're not, using only the things in your closet." She paused and then added, "Presented by 'the Spectre' in room 105. I think we've found our man."

"Wonderful," said Milos, as the words started going back to their previous language. "Do you know where this 'room 105' is, or when he is supposed to be giving this presentation?"

"Most of the people have been going down this hallway," noted Dantes, his eyes and a nod indicating which one he meant. "We can copy down what the number looks like now and search the hallway for it. As to when he will be in there, we will just have to wait and hope we haven't missed him."

The group was in luck. After only a cursory search, they found a room that had the designated numbers on a plate over the doorway. An elf was at the front of the room, speaking in a language they didn't understand.

"I don't think that's Elven she's speaking," said Ghorza.

"It's not," Dantes replied. "She's not an elf; she's just dressed like one."

"How do you know?" asked Ghorza.

"She doesn't smell like one, for one thing," Dantes explained. "Her ears aren't pointy enough for another."

"What does an elf smell like?" asked Ghorza as the door opened, and more people came in.

Dantes watched a young man walk by carrying a large bundle of clothing. "Tasty," he replied distractedly.

Milos noticed the object of Dantes' attention. "*It's him!*" he whispered. "It's the Spectre!"

The whisper was too loud, as the young man turned to peer at them through thick glasses, giving Dantes a chance to inspect him. The man was medium height and thin; he looked far too young and scrawny to be a warrior. In fact, he looked too scrawny to be much of anything except some sort of clerical transcriber in one of the new tax offices that had recently sprung up. Dantes shrugged. As he well knew, looks could be deceiving.

Not recognizing anyone in the group, the Spectre turned back and walked to the front row, where he took a seat and set down his bundle.

The not-elf must have asked for questions, because she was now talking back and forth with people in the audience. After a couple of minutes of this, the audience began slapping their hands together. Dantes thought that it looked like they were doing it in approval, so he joined in. Milos joined in making the slapping noise too, after Dantes elbowed him.

As the slapping noise ended, Dantes watched as many of the people in the audience got up and left the room, pushing past other people that were entering.

"I think he must be the next presenter," Ghorza said as the Spectre took the spot previously held by the not-elf.

Dantes smiled. "Yes, I believe so," he agreed. Ghorza had a knack for stating the obvious that rivaled her careless use of magic.

They watched as the Spectre began a demonstration of how to change a person's appearance. He started by showing the audience how to cut up black sheets to make a cloak that would render the wearer hard to see at night, and then he made masks out of an assortment of materials. He finished by showing the audience how to make themselves appear bigger than normal.

As he began the last topic, Milos whispered to Ghorza, "Aren't you going to cast a Translate spell so that we can understand him? This is exactly what he does back home. Maybe he will make a mistake and mention our world!"

"I don't have the manna to cast a Translate spell right now," Ghorza whispered back. "If I cast it, I will have to use some of my own life force, and I don't think it's worth three years of my life to hear what he is saying. It's obvious enough to me that he is the Spectre."

After a few more minutes there was another question and answer session, and then the people repeated the hand slapping. When they finished, the Spectre gathered up his materials and walked to the door, stopping to interact with several members of the audience on his way out.

Ghorza, Dantes and Milos got up and followed him out.

"What do you think?" asked Ghorza.

"I agree that he is the Spectre," Dantes replied. "I think we should follow him until he leads us back to his lair."

"I hope he goes to get some lunch," said Milos. "Can you do that trick again with the money?"

"No, I cannot," Ghorza answered. "Focus. Have you never missed a meal before?"

"Many times," replied Milos. "That doesn't mean that I want to do it again."

The group followed the Spectre for the remainder of the afternoon, splitting up from time to time so as not to draw his attention. The crowd was large enough that Milos and Ghorza were able to blend in fairly well; unfortunately, nearly everyone seemed to want to touch Dantes' horns. His mood worsened as the afternoon wore on.

The crowd started thinning as dinner time approached, and people went in search of their evening meals. Dantes sighed in relief as the Spectre finally left the area that the convention was using for its gathering. The group followed him through the building and into an open space that extended upwards over 100 feet. Looking up, they saw that they were in the largest building any of them had ever seen; there were at least ten floors above them.

"By the seventh level of hell," mumbled Ghorza. "What *is* this place?"

"It must be some sort of inn," guessed Dantes. "Look! The people on each level seem to be going into or coming out of rooms. The Spectre must be going to his room."

"Finally!" breathed Milos. "Maybe we can finally catch him and then get some dinner."

The group dropped back as the Spectre approached the open area, and they lost the cover and concealment of the crowd. The Spectre crossed the area without looking back, halting in front of a closed door. He pushed a button on the wall next to it that lit up. The group moved closer, so they could see what he was doing.

The door slid open, and several humans and an elf walked out of a small room. The Spectre walked in. "Let's follow him," Ghorza urged.

"No," Dantes disagreed. "We need to catch him with the crown, and it doesn't look like he has it. Let's wait and see if he comes back out. Maybe he's just going into another outhouse."

The door shut. A light above the door moved from left to right, illuminating various squiggles, some of which corresponded to the numbers they had seen previously. On the fifth squiggle the light paused, and then it went back to the left, pausing again on one of the others. When the light reached the left end, the door opened, and a number of people walked out. The Spectre wasn't one of them.

"You've lost him again!" hissed Milos.

A thought occurred to Dantes, and he ran back out into the open area. Looking up, a smile brightened his face for the first time that day. He motioned for the other two to join him, his face glowing.

"I take it that you had an idea," Ghorza said as she approached him. "Careful, you are about to catch fire."

Dantes went through a mental calming ritual, and his face lost its glow. Happily, he hadn't broken into full flame; *that* would have been difficult to explain.

"That is a magic room," Dantes said, pointing at the door that had closed again. "It has been enchanted with air magic to take people up to different levels and bring them back down. The button the Spectre pushed must have activated it. I saw him going into a room on the fifth level above us."

"Should we follow him up?" asked Ghorza. "He may have the crown in the room up there."

"Can you show me which room?" asked Milos. "I can try to find a bird or squirrel to look into it."

Dantes pointed to one of the rooms. Milos' eyes went blank as he searched the area for wildlife to use. Finally he nodded once and then seemed to sway back and forth as if gliding through the air. With a jolt, the swaying stopped. After a couple of seconds he started nodding as if lifting something with his mouth. Without warning, he jumped backward, and the light came back into his eyes.

"I found it!" Milos exclaimed. "He *is* the Spectre. The crown is on some sort of balcony in the back of his room, covered by a rag."

"Let's go get it back," said Dantes, fires raging in his eyes.

"I can probably use an air current to get up to his level," Ghorza said, gazing up at the Spectre's level, "but I can't get you up there, too."

"We'll take the magic room," Dantes said. He walked over to the door and pushed the same button the Spectre had pushed. The lights on top of the door moved from right to left. When the one on the left illuminated, the door opened.

The group walked into the room. After a pause, the door shut.

"Umm...now what?" asked Ghorza.

"We need to figure out the command words," said Dantes. "Go up!" Nothing happened.

"Rise!" tried Ghorza.

"Lift!" ordered Dantes.

"Maybe you have to say the command word in their language," guessed Ghorza.

"Can you use a Translate spell to translate our words into their language?" Dantes asked. "Maybe that would work."

"Maybe these buttons would work, too," said Milos, pointing to a row of buttons on the wall to the right of the door. "There are about as many buttons as the number of levels; each probably equates to a level."

"That actually makes sense," agreed Dantes with an approving nod. "The bottom one is probably our level. We want to go up five levels, so we need the button that is five above it." He counted up and said, "This one." He pushed the button, and the room started vibrating.

"I think we are going up," Dantes judged; "it feels like we are being pushed down toward the floor."

Just like on the outside, lights above the door illuminated as the magic room traveled up. With a small bump, the room stopped, and the door opened.

"That was fun," said Milos as the group exited. "I want to do it again."

"Focus," ordered Dantes, "This is where we finally catch him. Follow me." He led them to the room that he had seen the thief enter.

"Are you going to burn down the door or break it in?" asked Milos.

"Neither," said Dantes. "I will knock. When he opens the door, I will knock him to the ground, and Ghorza will use air shackles to hold him in place." Ghorza nodded. Of all of the things they had done and seen, this was the first thing that was familiar. Ghorza and Dantes had used this routine to capture a number of criminals.

"Ready?" asked Dantes. Ghorza nodded.

Dantes knocked on the door. The group could hear movement in the room, and then something passed in front of the peephole in the door. "Mmm bhsuejsh!" said a voice from the room. The person in the room walked away from the door.

Dantes knocked more insistently. The person came back to the door. "Mmm bhsuejsh!" said the voice from the room again, louder this time. The person started to leave.

Dantes knocked even harder on the door. This time the door opened a couple of inches to show a chain that ran across from the door to the doorjamb. "Mjm sdekar," the voice started to say, but it was interrupted as Dantes slammed open the door, using all of his considerable strength. The chain tore off, and the human was thrown backward to the floor.

"*Vincula!*" commanded Ghorza. Glowing chains of force appeared on the person, locking him to the floor. The group could see it was the Spectre. The door to the balcony was open, and a crown was on the room's large bed. A medium-sized mirror sat next to it, along with a small purse.

Dantes turned to Ghorza with a smile. "It has been a long time coming, but we've finally caught him. Red-handed, too." He turned to the Spectre. "What do you have to say for yourself?"

The Spectre stared at them, wild-eyed, and then said something in a foreign language.

"Of course he's going to pretend he doesn't speak our language now, too," said Milos, looking at the figure on the floor. The Spectre was naked, except for a small piece of cloth around his privates. "That's just pathetic."

"Well, we can fix that," answered Dantes. He glanced at his partner. "Ghorza, can you cast a Translate so that we can be done with this foolishness?"

"It will be my last Translate," replied Ghorza, "and I'm almost out of manna, too."

Dantes nodded. "That's fine," he said. "I think we're about done here."

"OK," she agreed. She pointed at the Spectre and commanded, "*Convertite.*"

"We finally have you," Dantes said, once the spell had taken effect. He nodded at the bed. "And with the crown still in your possession, too."

"That's not mine!" said the Spectre. "I never saw it before."

Dantes smiled. "I know it's not yours; it belongs to the queen. You stole it from her. I expect that the escape mirror sitting next to it isn't yours, either."

"No, none of that is mine," the Spectre said. "I just found it. Who are you people?"

"We're the ones that are here to bring you to justice," said Ghorza, "regardless of the games you play. First you don't speak our language. Now you're probably going to tell us you're not the Spectre, either, right?"

"Well yes, I go by the name 'Spectre,' but I didn't do anything. I didn't steal that crown."

Dantes smiled again. He enjoyed catching criminals. He couldn't torture them, but it was still a lot of fun to watch them squirm once they were caught. "Ghorza," he said, "would you please do the honors?"

"My pleasure," Ghorza said. "*Furta!*" she commanded with a snap. The crown glowed brilliantly, along with the purse that was sitting on the bed. She turned it over and dumped out a pile of gold coins. They glowed as well.

"The crown and the gold were all stolen," Dantes said, "and they were stolen by the Spectre."

"But I didn't do it," said the Spectre. "I don't know how those things got here."

"They never do," said Ghorza, shaking her head.

Dantes took off one of his boots. "Oops," he said as he smashed the mirror on the bed with it. "Seven years of bad luck for me; a lifetime of bad luck for you." He strapped his boot back on.

Milos scooped the coins back into the purse. "I claim these as my reward," he said. "You can have the crown; these are mine."

Dantes shrugged and looked at Ghorza. She shrugged back at him. "Fine," said Dantes, "I'm happy to get the crown back and strand him here." He turned to Ghorza. "How long will the chains last?"

"About an hour," Ghorza replied. "Long enough for us to get back and break the mirror, trapping him here forever."

"Good," said Dantes. "Let's go." He picked up the crown and turned to leave.

"I'm staying," said Milos, bouncing the purse in his hand so that the coins jingled. "I have money, and I like this world. The women are tall and pretty, and I'm rich. There are magic rooms to ride up and down in. This will be so much fun!"

Ghorza and Dantes looked at each other and shrugged again. "Works for me," said Dantes. "I'm happy to strand *you* here, too." The two magicians left, closing the door as they went out.

"Naughty, naughty, naughty," said Milos as he sat down on the bed. He shook his head. "You've been a very bad boy."

"But I didn't *do* anything!" the Spectre wailed. "I really didn't!"

"You can stop the denials," Milos said with a laugh. "I know you didn't do anything." He pulled a small mirror out of his bag and gazed into it, saying something that the Spectre strained to hear, but couldn't. The Spectre recoiled in horror as Milos' face melted, the flesh turning liquid and rearranging itself according to some predetermined pattern unknown to him. The result was sinister to behold.

"But, but, but, if you knew I didn't do it, why didn't you tell them?" asked the Spectre, his brain refusing to accept what his eyes had just seen.

"That wouldn't have been very smart," Milos replied, patting his face into place as it hardened, "since I was the one that really *did* take them." He got up. "That reminds me."

Milos walked out onto the balcony and pulled a handful of shelled peanuts from a pocket. Placing them on the table, he waved over the railing. Within seconds, a flock of crows flew in and started feeding. "Thank you for bringing those things up for me," he said, stroking the one closest to him.

"So you are just using me to take the blame?" asked the Spectre as Milos returned to the room.

"Of course I am," replied Milos. "You are as stupid as those other two fools. They got so excited to see the crown that they will take it back to our world and destroy their one way of coming back here before they realize it's a fake. You're helping me start my new life."

"But, didn't they do some sort of spell or something to see if the crown was stolen?"

"Of course they did," replied Milos. "They checked it the same way they always do, which is why I had the forgery made out of the gold and gems that I had stolen previously. It glowed like it was stolen by me, because it *was* stolen by me...just not from the time and the place they thought it was." He pulled a crown from his bag. The gems shone with an internal light and brilliance that the other crown didn't have. Milos smiled. The queen's crown was more valuable than anything he had ever seen or held. Not only was it worth a fortune, Milos knew that it also held a significance that dwarfed its monetary value.

Milos' laugh was gleeful and maniacal at the same time, leading the Spectre to believe that the person he was dealing with was not entirely balanced. He didn't like where that led his thinking.

"Wha...what are you going to do with me?" he asked.

"With you?" asked Milos with a laugh as he walked over to gaze at his reflection in the mirror on the dresser. He pulled a chair over and reached forward to adjust something on the mirror. "Nothing. You are trivial to my plans. No one in my world knows you exist, and no one in this world will believe you if you tell them about me."

The Spectre knew he was right. Anyone that came in and saw him chained to the floor would think that it was some sort of sexual tryst gone bad, not a case of inter-dimensional theft and recovery. He could never tell anyone about this; they would lock him away forever. "But what about you?" he asked. "What are you going to do?"

Milos smiled as he stepped up onto the chair. "What am I going to do?" he asked. "Anything I want to." He stepped through the mirror and was gone.

# # # # #

The following is an
Excerpt from Book 1 of the War for Dominance:

Can't Look Back

Chris Kennedy

Available from Chris Kennedy Publishing

eBook, Paperback and Audio Book

Excerpt from "Can't Look Back"

John walked back to the mirror with a new purpose and pressed the buttons from right to left, then jumped backwards as the mirror shimmered. The glass now looked...fluid, somehow. He reached out to touch it with the index finger on his right hand, noticing that his finger didn't shake this time. He touched the mirror and found that it was no longer solid. His finger went into it. He could feel a tug on his finger, pulling him in.

He tried to pull his finger back out, but couldn't. The tug became more insistent, pulling his hand up into his wrist. He braced himself on the dresser, bent over at the waist. The lower half of his body kept him from being pulled any further into the mirror, but the pull only got stronger. His arm felt like it was going to be pulled from the socket, and there was no sign that it was letting up. The pull became stronger still, and John cried out as the pain in his shoulder became overwhelming.

He didn't know where the mirror led. He didn't know what would happen to him there. All he knew was that the pain was blinding, and he was about to lose his arm. A tear rolled down his cheek. He pulled the desk chair over with his right foot and stood up on it. The pain lessened as his arm went further into the mirror. The pull was unrelenting, though, and it again began drawing him further into the mirror. With no other options, he put his left arm up to the mirror like he was diving into a pool. It was drawn into the mirror the same way that his right arm had been. He leaned forward and pushed off the chair.

The mirror consumed him. He was gone.

* * * * *

ABOUT THE AUTHOR

A bestselling Science Fiction/Fantasy author and speaker, Chris Kennedy is a former naval aviator with over 3,000 hours flying attack and reconnaissance aircraft. Chris is currently working as an Instructional Systems Designer for the Navy.

Chris' full length novels on Amazon include the "Occupied Seattle" military fiction duology ("Red Tide: The Chinese Invasion of Seattle" and "Occupied Seattle") and "The Theogony" science fiction trilogy ("Janissaries," "When the Gods Aren't Gods" and "Terra Stands Alone"). Chris has also released "Can't Look Back," the first book of the "War for Dominance" fantasy trilogy.

Additional Titles by Chris Kennedy:

"Red Tide: The Chinese Invasion of Seattle"

"Occupied Seattle"

"Janissaries: Book One of the Theogony"

"When the Gods Aren't Gods: Book Two of the Theogony"

"Terra Stands Alone: Book Three of the Theogony"

"Can't Look Back: Book One of the War for Dominance"

"Self-Publishing for Profit: How to Get Your Book Out of Your Head and Into the Stores"

* * * * *

Connect with Chris Kennedy Online:

Facebook: https://www.facebook.com/chriskennedypublishing.biz

Blog: http://chriskennedypublishing.com/

Want to be immortalized in a future book?
Join the Red Shirt List on the blog!